Performing Artist Se

FRÉDÉRIC CHOPIN
Piano Works
Edited by Joseph Banowetz

DEDICATION

This volume is for Adam Wodnicki, great Chopin interpreter and loyal friend.

Project Manager: DALE TUCKER
Art Design: LISA GREENE MANE

ONTENTS

Page No.   Track No.

$\mathcal{A}$BOUT THE EDITOR

JOSEPH BANOWETZ has been described in *Fanfare Record Review* (U.S.) as "a giant among keyboard artists of our time," and by *Russia's News* (Moscow) as "a magnificent virtuoso." He has been heard as recitalist and orchestral soloist on five continents, with guest appearances in recent seasons with such orchestras as the St. Petersburg (formerly the Leningrad) Philharmonic, the New Zealand Symphony (in a twelve-concert national tour), the Prague Radio Symphony, the Moscow State Symphony, the Belarus National Philharmonic of Minsk, the Hong Kong Philharmonic, the Shanghai Symphony, and the Beijing Central Philharmonic.

Banowetz has received international critical acclaim for his series of compact disc recordings for the Marco Polo, Naxos, and Altarus labels. His world-premiere recording of Balakirev works received a German Music Critics' outstanding record of the year award, and his world-premiere recording of Anton Rubinstein's Concertos Nos. 1 and 2 received a similar citation from *Fanfare Record Review* (U.S.). He has recorded twenty-two compact discs including concertos of Tchaikovsky's, Liszt's, and d'Albert's and the world-premiere recordings of all eight of the Anton Rubinstein works for piano and orchestra. Banowetz has recorded with the Moscow Symphony, the Slovak State Radio Orchestra, the Czecho-Slovak State Philharmonic, the Budapest Symphony, the Beijing Central Opera Orchestra, and the Hong Kong Philharmonic.

A graduate with a First Prize from the Vienna Academy for Music and Dramatic Arts, Banowetz also studied with Carl Friedberg (a pupil of Clara Schumann's) and Gÿorgy Sándor (a pupil of Béla Bartók's). In addition to his performance and recording activities, he has given lectures and masterclassses at such schools as Juilliard in New York City, the St. Petersburg Conservatory, the Royal College of Music in London, the Beijing Central Conservatory, the Shanghai Conservatory, and the Hong Kong Academy for the Performing Arts.

Banowetz has been invited to serve on many international piano competition juries, these having included the Gina Bachauer International Piano Competition (U.S.), 2001 World Piano Competition (U.S.), the Arthur Rubinstein International Piano Master Competition (Israel), the Scottish International Piano Competition (Glasgow), and the PTNA Young Artists Competition (Japan). His award-winning book *The Pianist's Guide to Pedaling* has been printed in five languages. In 1992 Banowetz was presented with the Liszt Medal by the Hungarian Liszt Society in Budapest. Mr. Banowetz is a Steinway artist.

Presently Banowetz is on the Artist Piano Faculty of the University of North Texas.

BOUT THIS COLLECTION

The pieces in this collection have been carefully chosen to introduce players to a fascinating range of works—from Chopin's earliest published composition to those only finally put into print after his death under the supervision of his pupil, Julian Fontana. Some of Chopin's most beautiful works are in this collection.

Chopin's original markings have been carefully left untouched, with a few supplementary performance suggestions having been added by the editor when those by Chopin seemed incomplete or needing clarification for the less experienced performer. Chopin's pedaling indications are often based on the old so-called "rhythmic" form of notation, where the pedal is lifted before, not as, a new harmony is played. According to Moriz Rosenthal (1862–1946)—who was not only a pupil of Liszt's but also of Karol Mikuli's, Chopin's student—this form of pedaling gave way to our modern so-called *legato* pedaling technique only around the end of the third quarter of the nineteenth century. For this reason, the editor has clarified all pedaling indications according to modern notation. Accompanying each piece are study suggestions that will help the performer anticipate a few of the problems that many pianists encounter when first learning these beautiful works. In some cases, Chopin's own fingerings, most of them found in pupils' study copies, have been kept.

PERFORMANCE SUGGESTIONS FOR INDIVIDUAL CHOPIN PIECES

Mazurka in B♭ Major, Op. Posth. 7, No. 1:
This Mazurka was first published in Paris in 1832 but may actually have been composed earlier.

Measures 1–24: Play each sixteenth lightly, always feeling it belongs and leads to the next longer note.

Measures 29–31: Do not use pedal in these measures. Play a slightly faster tempo, and place light accents on each left-hand chord so as to give a subtle two-plus-three feeling against the right-hand melody.

Mazurka in G Minor, Op. Posth. 67, No. 2:
Measures 1–16: Carefully shaping the ends of the slurs with a slight lifting of the wrist will help convey the mazurka-like rhythmic "lilt" contained in the music. Chopin often uses slurs not only to indicate a shaping of notes within a phrase, but to show a slight *rubato* as well.

Measures 21–24: Play the triplets very lightly. They should lead slightly to each second beat.

Mazurka in A Minor, Op. Posth. 67, No. 4:
Measures 18–20: Releasing the pedal on the second beats will give a lilt to the rhythm, especially if this is followed by a characteristic light accent on the third beats. Some performers will also slightly quicken the triplets in these bars. All of these subtle nuances will help give a dance-like mazurka feeling rather than just sounding like a regular piece in three-four time.

Mazurka in F Major, Op. Posth. 68, No. 3:

In this mazurka, the accents shift lightly back and fourth from the second and third beats. For instance, measures 1, 3, 5, 6, and 7 should receive light accents on the third beats, and measures 2, 4, and 8 on the second beats.

Measures 33–44: Make clear the light accents given by Chopin in the left hand. These greatly help project this passage's mazurka rhythm and style, especially characterized by the drone bass below the melody in Lydian mode with the raised fourth-degree scale step.

Cantabile in B♭ Major:

Measures 1–12: The dots occurring on the lowest left-hand notes in each of these measures stand for light accents, not *staccato* touches. See the discussion for similar passages in Nocturne in E♭ Major, Op. 9, No. 2, elsewhere in this edition.

Measure 2: Catch the pedal with the final note following the ornament. Similarly in measure 6, do not allow the B♭ grace note to be held in the pedal.

Nocturne in C♯ Minor:

Four versions, none printed during Chopin's lifetime, exist of this nocturne. Written in 1830, it bears the inscription "To my sister, Ludwika, for practice before she starts playing my concerto." The title Nocturne in C♯ Minor was added later by Ludwika. Some of the melodic material is closely related to Chopin's Concerto in F Minor, Op. 21, which was composed around this time. This nocturne also contains allusions to Chopin's song *Maiden's Wish*. The present edition is based on a fair copy of a later final autographed version that was subsequently lost.

Measures 33–43: This section contains characteristic features of the mazurka. Pay close attention to the recurring accents on the second beats, and keep the triplets light and dance-like.

Measures 57 and 60: Make a distinction in touch between the *legato* and *portato* parts of each right-hand scale passage, for even though pedal is used, this distinction will change the sound as well as allow for a slight *rubato.*

Nocturne in E♭ Major, Op. 9, No. 2:

This is a youthful, yet deservedly famous, work written sometime before 1832. Over the years, Chopin taught it to many pupils, at times writing in fingerings as well as a number of variants and embellished passage work. The present edition, although based on the earliest printed editions, includes subsequent fingering additions made by Chopin. They should be tried out because they often give an indication of the sound, and even subtle *rubato,* Chopin may have wished. See, in particular, measures 14, 16, and 26. In measure 16, note both the *portato* touch and original fingering, which are especially clear examples of such careful distinctions of sound and *rubato* made by the composer.

Measure 1 and throughout: The left-hand dots stand for light accents, not real staccatos. This dual meaning of the dot was common in piano music of this period and was used frequently by such composers as Beethoven and Schubert. See also the Cantabile in B♭ Major, found elsewhere in this edition for another example of this usage of the dot.

Measures 13 and 21: The dotted lines are indications given in pupils' copies by Chopin that the right-hand arpeggios are to be played on the beat. Since most listeners will still hear the top G as coming on the downbeat, do not subtract the length of time needed to play the small notes from the high G, but simply "steal" a little time and give the G its full value.

Sostenuto in E♭ Major:

The original manuscript of this untitled work is dated July 20, 1840, and was found written in an album owned by Emile Gaillard, a pupil of Chopin's.

Measures 3, 11, 19, 20 and 23: If wished, all of the small notes can be played on the beat. If this is done, measure 23, for example, would be played as follows:

Ex. 1:

The important matter in any case is that the small notes do not obstruct the long flow of melodic line.

Measures 17–24: Think of this section as being a wonderful cello solo played by someone like Mstislav Rostropovich.

Polonaise in G Minor:

This, the first of Chopin's polonaises, was written in 1817 and published when the composer was only seven years old. A facsimile of the only known copy was first published in 1930. Both the mazurka and polonaise are dances from Chopin's homeland, and he would use their rhythms to great effect in a good number of his works. A common polonaise rhythm is as follows:

Ex. 2:

To help project this rhythm, keep the sixteenths very light, feeling that they always slightly lead to the next eighth note. Under no circumstances should either of the sixteenths be stressed or sluggishly played. Some performers when playing a polonaise compress the rhythm of the sixteenths in an effective and idiomatic manner, approximately as follows:

Ex. 3:

For many performers, simply making a small *crescendo* through the two sixteenths will create a similar effect. This characteristic polonaise rhythm occurs in measures 3 and 15.

Chopin's Préludes, Op. 28, were written for the most part during the winter of 1838–39, at the time when he and George Sand, as well as her son Maurice and daughter Solange, were living together at the abandoned monastery of Valdemosa on the Balearic island of Majorca, Spain. These preludes are among Chopin's most imaginative works, each being a miniature tone poem that captures a central mood or image, often at an extreme level of emotional intensity.

Prélude in E Minor, Op. 28, No. 4:

It is common to hear this prelude played too slowly so that a long phrase line cannot be maintained. Much of this prelude contains a pedaling problem found in many works that have a repeated chord or single note accompaniment to the melody. In the present instance, as the pedal is raised on each change of harmony in either the right or left hand, make certain there is not a momentary gap in the left-hand repeated chord figuration. Keep the chords as *legato* as possible with the fingers by not letting the keys come up all the way to the top, so as to maintain a one-note *legato* on repeated notes. This will help ensure that a break between the chords is not heard as the pedal is changed.

Measures 16–17: Make certain to achieve a clear dynamic (and emotional) climax with the high C in measure 17. Use the *stretto* (quickening of the tempo) starting in measure 16 to lead to this.

Measure 23: Wait a good length of time on the *fermata,* and then play the final chords like a sad farewell.

Prélude in B Minor, Op. 28, No. 6:

Some feel that this prelude, as with Prélude, Op. 28, No. 15, has an equal claim to being nicknamed the *Raindrop Prélude.*

Measures 1–6 and 9–26: Lightly accent the first of each pair of eighth notes, mimicking the sound of slow drops of water or a faint bell tolling in the distance. You can help maintain the hypnotic stressing of the first note of each pair of eighths by slightly dropping your wrist on the first note and then raising it gently as the second note is played more softly. "Orchestrate" the music by imitating the sound of a fine cello with your left hand.

Prélude in A Major, Op. 28, No. 7:

Do not overly sentimentalize this lovely miniature mazurka-like work, and take Chopin's *andantino* indication literally.

The long pedalings throughout this piece are needed to sustain the low downbeat bass notes and will work best in a larger hall on a concert instrument. Do not accent the right-hand downbeat notes so as to enable them to blend into the larger stretches of pedal.

Prélude in C Minor, Op. 28, No. 20:

Measures 1–4: A common error is to "flip" the pedal rapidly up and down on each new chord. In particular, when playing at a fairly high dynamic level on a larger concert instrument, the dampers need more time to stop the ringing from each preceding harmony. Leave the dampers on the strings at each new pedal change for about an eighth-note of time to ensure a completely clear change of harmony when the pedal is then re-depressed.

Measure 3: According to the Oxford edition, the flat before the E on the fourth beat was added by Chopin in a study score of Jane Stirling's, a pupil from Scotland and one of the composer's most loyal friends.

Waltz in D♭ Major, Op. 64, No. 1:

This famous work is dedicated to Countess Delfina Potocka. According to Frederick Niecks, an early biographer of Chopin, it was inspired by the beautiful countess's dog Marquis going round and round in an attempt to catch its tail.

Although nicknamed the *Minute Waltz,* do not try to make your interpretation a speed contest! For example, the following outstanding Chopin players take considerably longer by choice: Alfred Cortot, 1 minute 35 seconds; Dinu Lipatti, 1 minute 42 seconds; Sergei Rachmaninoff, 1 minute 56 seconds; and Artur Rubinstein, 1 minute 48 seconds.

Measure 38: The use of the word *sostenuto* often means a slight sustaining (holding back) of the tempo as well as implies a sustained, legato manner of playing.

Measure 45: A four-against-three rhythm usually creates problems. Chopin's own *Fantaisie-Impromptu,* Opus Posth. 66, is a famous example. To solve this problem, some performers subdivide the note values into the lowest common denominator, counting as follows:

Ex. 4:

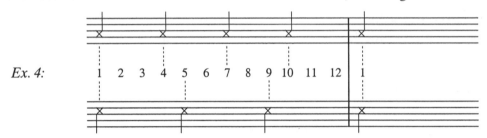

Others use words to roughly match the rhythm. The editor has always found it easier to simply learn each hand alone perfectly and in tempo. (Unlike a two-against-three rhythm that becomes easier the slower it is played, a three-against-four rhythm becomes harder the slower it is played.) Then play the hands together in tempo, always aiming for the next beat where the hands play a note exactly together.

Waltz in C♯ Minor, Op. 64, No. 2:

Measures 3, 4, 7, 8, and later similar passages: Play the grace notes as follows:

Ex. 5:

Measures 1–8 and later similar passages: Lifting the pedal about a sixteenth note of time early at the end of each measure gives this and similar passages a sort of waltz "lilt." Keep the right hand as *legato* as possible.

Measures 33–36 and later similar passages: Lift the pedal just after playing the left-hand chord on each third beat. Then, when this section is repeated more softly and lightly, release the pedal on each second beat.

Measure 84: Do not play this measure, as many do, in the following manner:

Ex. 6:

Rather bring in the left hand approximately as follows, still playing freely to avoid a feeling of squareness. This is a good example of how Chopin deliberately avoids the following too-easy solution that destroys any feeling of free *rubato*.

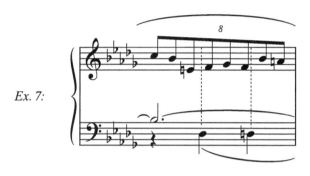

Ex. 7:

Measures 112–124: Many pianists lightly emphasize the thumb in each right-hand figuration. This gives a subtle feeling of variety to a passage that is repeated several times. (See Example 8.)

Ex. 8:

Waltz in B Minor, Op. Posth. 69, No. 2:

Measures 1–4, 9–12, and later similar passages: This lovely work has a characteristic "drooping" shape to the melody. It is important to always show the diminuendo, which underlines this expressive characteristic of the melody.

Waltz in A Minor, Op. Posth.:

It is possible that this work, which was published only after Chopin's death, may have been written as early as 1831, perhaps during Chopin's trip to Vienna.

Lifting the pedal throughout on the second beat of almost each measure will help maintain a feeling of elegance and lightness. Slightly longer pedaling should be used only in measures 21 and 56.

Valse Mélancolique in F♯ Minor:

This lovely, lesser-known work probably dates from 1838–39, during the time spent by Chopin and George Sand in Majorca. Throughout, lightly stress each left-hand downbeat note so that it can support both the melody and accompaniment harmony. Chopin specifically indicates this in measures 24–54 with the double stemming of the left-hand downbeats, where in the slower *poco più lento* tempo, it becomes even more important to maintain the bass line.

*L*IFE OF CHOPIN

Frédéric François Chopin, along with Franz Liszt, is generally regarded as one of the most original pianists and composers of all time, whose playing and manner of writing for the instrument revolutionized the music of the day. Born March 1, 1810, some twenty miles west of Warsaw in the small village of Żelazowa Wola, his father Nicolas was of French descent and his mother Polish. A sister had been born three years earlier, and two other sisters would arrive within the next three years. In the October following Frédéric's birth, the family moved to Warsaw, where Nicolas took on a new post as teacher at the Lyceum.

Chopin was extraordinarily precocious both musically and intellectually and soon became a frequent guest performer in the homes of the Warsaw aristocracy. He began composing at the age of seven, and his first published work was the *Polonaise in G Minor* included in this volume. Chopin was given an excellent general and musical education, with his piano instruction coming first from Wojciech Żywny and then from Józef Elsner, the German-born director of the Warsaw Conservatory. Upon his successful graduation in the late spring of 1829, Chopin decided to expand his professional opportunities by performing two well-received concerts in Vienna. Returning for a short time to Warsaw for some further appearances, Chopin finally left Poland November 2, 1830, bound for Paris, which was then the musical capital of Europe. He would never again see Poland.

When Chopin first arrived unknown and without many friends in Paris, he understandably was unsure of both himself and his future. For a brief time he seriously considered taking piano lessons from Friedrich Kalkbrenner, one of the most celebrated pianists and teachers of the day in Paris. But he soon recovered from the initial shock of Parisian cultural life and quickly abandoned this idea. February 26, 1832, Chopin gave his first concert in Paris. From then until the end of his life, he was a favorite in both the highest cultural and aristocratic circles of Paris. Chopin was slight of build. He was of medium height, weighed about a hundred pounds during his years of relative health (he may have already been in the early stages of tuberculosis), and had gray eyes, fair hair, and delicate aristocratic features. His manners were as impeccable as his dress, which was quietly elegant and always in step with the most up-to-date Parisian fashions. But behind the public image of elegant reserve and politeness were coarseness and an often-cruel intolerance for many of his acquaintances, which he revealed frequently in letters to trusted Polish friends. In his dealings with publishers, he soon came to be ruthless and cynical. Chopin first met Liszt in 1831. Their friendship was at best a love-hate one, for although Chopin on occasion grudgingly admitted Liszt's prowess as a performer before the large public, he detested his compositions, as he did those by Schumann, Berlioz, and, to a lesser extent, Mendelssohn. Chopin's enthusiasm for opera, however, remained unquenched until the end of his life.

Soon after his arrival in Paris, Chopin was quickly able to build a full piano class, the majority of which consisted of wealthy ladies of the aristocracy who could pay his enormous fees. Unlike Liszt, who much later would teach some of the most important pianists of the next generation, Chopin had relatively few students who developed major careers. The lone exception was the remarkably gifted prodigy Karl Filtsch, whose death in 1845 at the age of fifteen robbed the musical world both of a potentially major pianist and the one member of Chopin's class who might have carried on a genuine Chopin tradition as a public performer. A few others such as Georges Mathias (1826–1910) and Karol Mikuli (1821–1897) had distinguished careers primarily as teachers.

In 1836 Chopin was introduced by Liszt to Aurore Dudevant, one of the most prolific novelists of the time. Better known today by her pen name of George Sand (it was then unfashionable for a woman to write under her real name), she at the age of thirty-two was a divorcée with two children, equally famous both for her enormously popular novels and talked-about love affairs. The younger Chopin, on the other hand, was relatively inexperienced. But by 1838, Sand and Chopin were openly living together and evidently very much in love. Deciding to spend the winter of 1838–1839 away from Paris, Chopin, Sand, and her two children, Maurice and Solange, embarked for the Spanish island of Majorca, where they rented a wing of an abandoned monastery. Soon the initial idyllic journey turned to stark reality. The residents of the island were openly hostile because of suspicions of Chopin's illness. The monastery itself was located on a plateau between the mountains and open sea, which allowed both wind and rain to turn everything into a damp, chilled hell. Chopin wrote in a letter to his pupil Julian Fontana: "The cell has the shape of a tall tomb . . . one can shout . . . still silence!" Chopin began to have morbid hallucinations, and Sand years later wrote that "For him the cloister was full of terrors and phantoms, even when he felt well . . . . I would find him at ten o'clock at night, pale at his piano, with haunted eyes, and hair standing on end." They were able to stand it only for some fourteen weeks, after which they moved, first to Marseilles and then to Sand's country home in Nohant. There Chopin made an outwardly excellent recovery during the summer of 1839.

For the next seven years, Chopin's life settled into a largely predictable pattern. During the winters he was caught up in a busy round of attending concerts and operas, social events, and, of course, a heavy teaching load. The summers were spent with Sand in Nohant. As a public performer, Chopin was heard but a total of some thirty times in concert during his entire life. The majority of his appearances that built his fame were informal ones in the homes of the aristocracy. He once wrote to Liszt: "I am not at all fit for giving concerts, for the crowd intimidates me, its breath suffocates me, I feel paralyzed by its curious look, and the unknown faces make me dumb." In spite of his busy schedule and ever-declining health, Chopin continued to write masterpiece after masterpiece. Notoriously exacting, he at times spent many months over a single work. His music by this time was in hot demand by publishers not only in France, but in Germany and England as well. Chopin constantly seemed to revise his scores even after publication so that there never seemed to be a "final" edition. Although encouraged by his teacher Elsner to write an opera, Chopin early on sensed that with the exception of a few small songs, an early trio, and a magnificent late sonata for cello, the piano would remain his only compositional outlet.

By 1847, his relationship with Sand had progressively been deteriorating and had been punctuated by arguments and intense strain from both sides. A final break was precipitated in 1847 when Chopin took Sand's daughter's side in a bitter family argument. Sand saw him only once more when they briefly met by accident a year later. Sand later wrote: "I saw him again for an instant in March, 1848. I pressed his trembling and icy hand. I wished to speak to him, he slipped away!" At the time of his breakup with Sand, Chopin was both terminally ill and mentally exhausted. After a final concert February 16, 1848, in Paris, Chopin was persuaded by a wealthy pupil to undertake a tour of England and Scotland. Jane Stirling (1804–1859) had studied with Chopin for about four years. Tracing her descent from a wealthy and distinguished family in Scotland, Stirling was undoubtedly in love with Chopin. He, on the other hand, badly needed additional money by that time, so he took on the tour. Being dragged from city to city, where he didn't know the language, to perform with varying degrees of public success caused him to become progressively more ill. After a concert in Manchester, following a performance of his so-called *Funeral March Sonata,* Op. 35, he wrote to Solange that he saw "those accursed creatures which had appeared to me one lugubrious night at the Chartreuse (in Majorca). I had to leave for one instant to pull myself together, after which I continued without saying anything." In another letter he asks, "Why doesn't God finish me off at once instead of killing me by inches?"

Chopin's return to Paris November 24 found him too ill to teach, compose, or perform. Debts accumulated alarmingly, which, mercifully, Jane Stirling anonymously helped pay. The end came the evening of October 17, 1849, after days of agony. He was buried in Paris's Père-Lachaise Cemetary. By the time of his death, Liszt's observation in 1841 that "A complete silence of criticism already reigns about him, as if posterity already had come" was now a reality.

$\mathscr{S}$UGGESTIONS FOR FURTHER READING

The literature about Chopin is diverse and fascinating. An acquaintance with some of the references below will vastly help in gaining an understanding of Chopin's multi-faceted genius.

Eigeldinger, Jean-Jacques. *Chopin: Pianist and Teacher, as Seen by His Pupils.* Cambridge, Cambridge University Press, 1986. (This is one of the most important pieces of Chopin research to have been released, for it gathers together an incredible amount of material coming from people who actually knew the composer. A must for all serious Chopin students!)

Hinson, Maurice. "Pedaling the Piano Works of Chopin." Chapter in *The Pianist's Guide to Pedaling* by Joseph Banowetz. Bloomington, Indiana University Press, 1985. (A comprehensive examination of Chopin's pedaling based on original manuscripts.)

Methuen-Campbell, James. *Chopin Playing From the Composer to the Present Day.* New York, Taplinger Publishing Co., Inc., 1981. (This is an in-depth discussion of Chopin's performance style, based on a wide examination of recordings, including those of pianists who studied with pupils of Chopin's. A most valuable resource work.)

Niecks, Frederick. *Frederick Chopin as a Man and Musician,* 2 volumes. Paganiniana Publications, Neptune City, ND. (This is a famous pioneering work on Chopin, which remains extremely important because of Niecks' having had access to many people still living at the time of original publication [1888] who had personally known the composer.)

Szulc, Tad. *Chopin in Paris: The Life and Times of the Romantic Composer.* New York, A Lisa Drew Book/Scribner, 1998. (This is a superb, highly readable recent biography that examines and clarifies many aspects of Chopin's complex personality.)

Walker, Alan. *Chopin: Profiles of the Man and the Musician.* Barrie and Rockliff, London, 1966. (A collection of essays on specialized aspects of Chopin as composer and performer by various Chopin authorities.)

Pencil portrait by George Sand, 1841.

MAZURKA IN B-FLAT MAJOR

OP. 7, NO. 1

FRÉDÉRIC CHOPIN
Edited by Joseph Banowetz

* The metronome indication is from the first printed edition, published c. 1833 by Carl Friedrich Kistner in Leipzig.

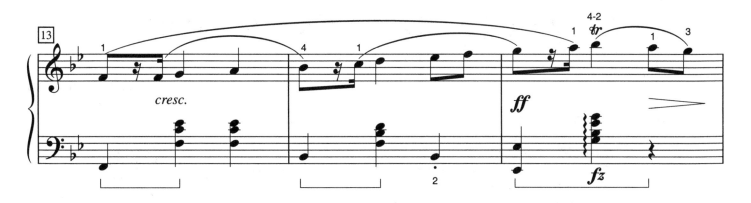

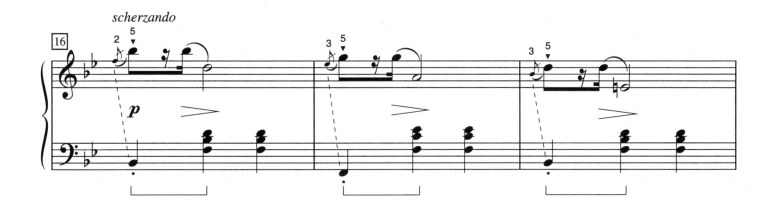

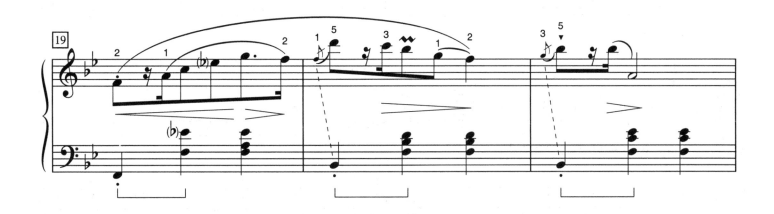

Mazurka in B-Flat Major,
Op. 7, No. 1 - 4 - 2
ELM00043

4

Mazurka in B-Flat Major,
Op. 7, No. 1 - 4 - 3
ELM00043

MAZURKA IN G MINOR

OP. 67, NO. 2

FRÉDÉRIC CHOPIN
Edited by Joseph Banowetz

Cantabile (M.M. ♩ = 144)*

* The metronome indication is found in the 1855 first edition published by A.M. Schlesinger, as edited by Julian Fontana.

Mazurka in G Minor,
Op. 67, No. 2 - 3 - 2
ELM00043

MAZURKA IN A MINOR
OP. 67, NO. 4

FRÉDÉRIC CHOPIN
Edited by Joseph Banowetz

* The Allegretto indication is given in the autograph. The 1855 first edition published by A.M. Schlesinger, as edited by Julian Fontana, gives a tempo indication of *Moderato animato*, ♩ = 138.

Mazurka in A Minor,
Op. 67, No. 4 - 3 - 1
ELM00043

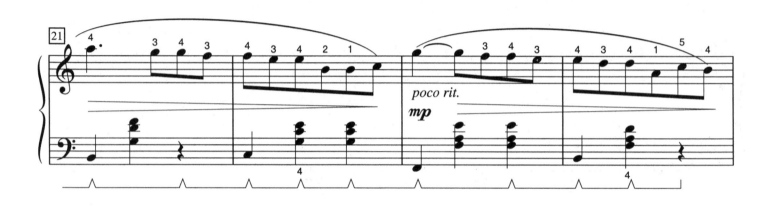

MAZURKA IN F MAJOR

OP. 68, NO. 3

FRÉDÉRIC CHOPIN
Edited by Joseph Banowetz

Allegro, ma non troppo (M.M. ♩ = 132*)

* The metronome indication is found in the 1855 first edition published by A.M. Schlesinger, as edited by Jules Fontana.

Mazurka in F Major,
Op. 68, No. 3 - 3 - 1
ELM00043

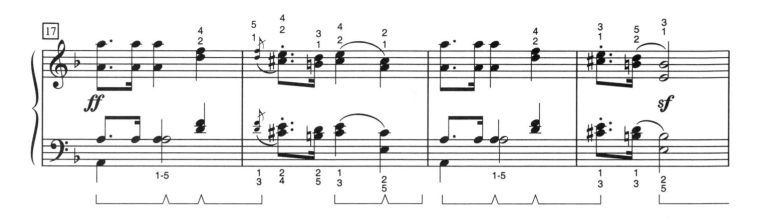

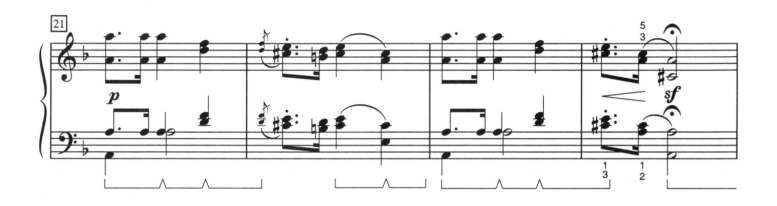

Mazurka in F Major,
Op. 68, No. 3 - 3 - 2
ELM00043

Poco più vivo

Tempo I

D.S. ℅ al Fine

CANTABILE IN B-FLAT MAJOR

KK IVB/6, BI 17

FRÉDÉRIC CHOPIN
Edited by Joseph Banowetz

* There is no tempo indication given by the composer.

Cantabile in B-Flat Major,
KK IVB/16, BI 17 - 1 - 1
ELM00043

NOCTURNE IN C-SHARP MINOR

BI 49, KK IVA/IB

FRÉDÉRIC CHOPIN
Edited by Joseph Banowetz

Lento, con gran espressione (M.M. ♩ = 60-63)

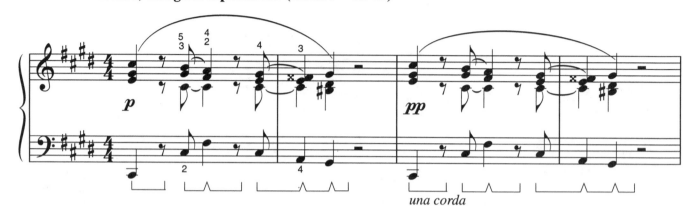

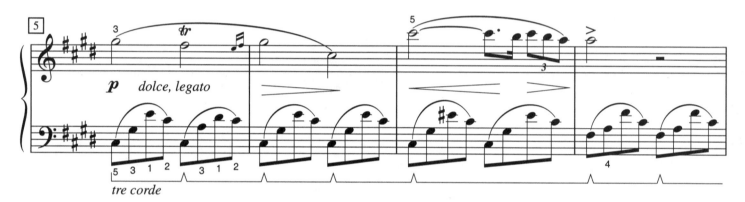

Nocturne in C-Sharp Minor, BI 49, KK IVA/IB - 4 - 1
ELM00043

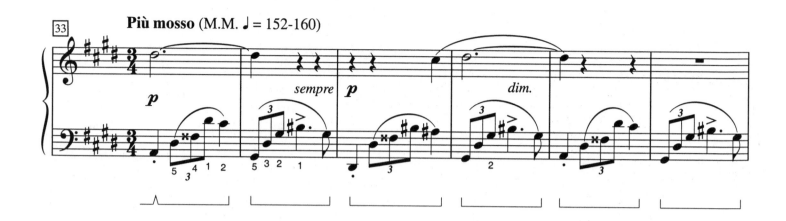

Nocturne in C-Sharp Minor, BI 49, KK IVA/IB - 4 - 4
ELM00043

NOCTURNE IN E-FLAT MAJOR
OP. 9, NO. 2

FRÉDÉRIC CHOPIN
Edited by Joseph Banowetz

* This is the composer's own metronome indication. Many performers will feel this to be a bit rapid, and may prefer something closer to ♪ = 108-112.

** Chopin's original fingerings are given in italics. Unusual as some of them may at first seem, they often convey a subtle change of touch, as well as a slight rubato within the phrasing.

Nocturne in E-Flat Major, Op. 9, No. 2 - 4 - 3
ELM00043

Nocturne in E-Flat Major, Op. 9, No. 2 - 4 - 4
ELM00043

SOSTENUTO IN E-FLAT MAJOR

KK IVB/10, BI 133

FRÉDÉRIC CHOPIN
Edited by Joseph Banowetz

* Play the small note in this bar, as well as those found in bars 11, 19, 20, and 23, very rapidly and lightly before the beat.
  Keep the eighth-notes on either side of the small notes as legato as possible.

Sostenuto in E-Flat Major,
KK IVB/10, BI 133 - 1 - 1
ELM00043

POLONAISE IN G MINOR

BI 1

FRÉDÉRIC CHOPIN
Edited by Joseph Banowetz

* **Allegro maestoso** (M.M. ♩ = 92-96)

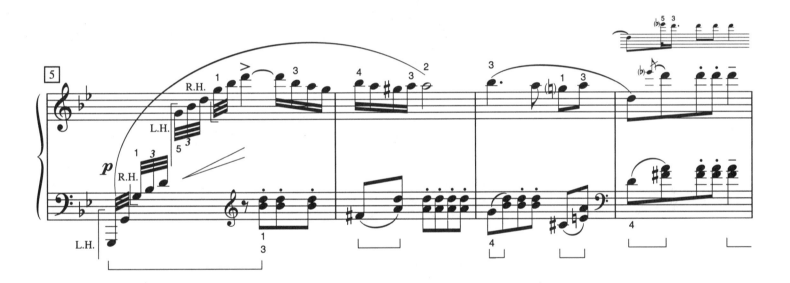

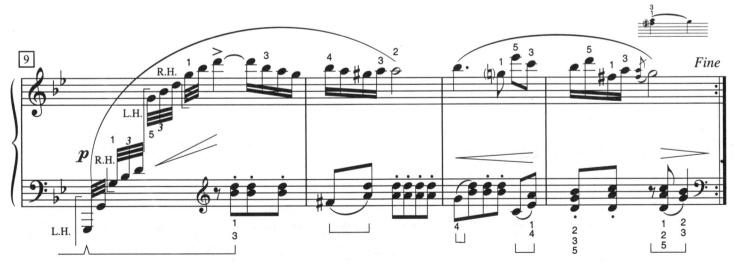

* There is no tempo indication in the original score.

Polonaise in G Minor, BI 1 - 3 - 2
ELM00043

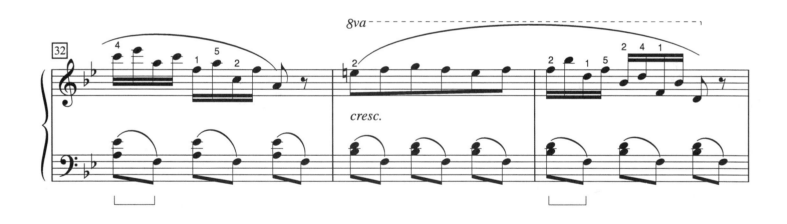

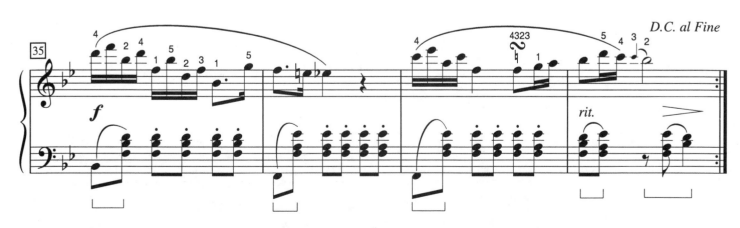

PRÉLUDE IN E MINOR

OP. 28, NO. 4

FRÉDÉRIC CHOPIN
Edited by Joseph Banowetz

Largo (M.M. ♩ = 72-76)

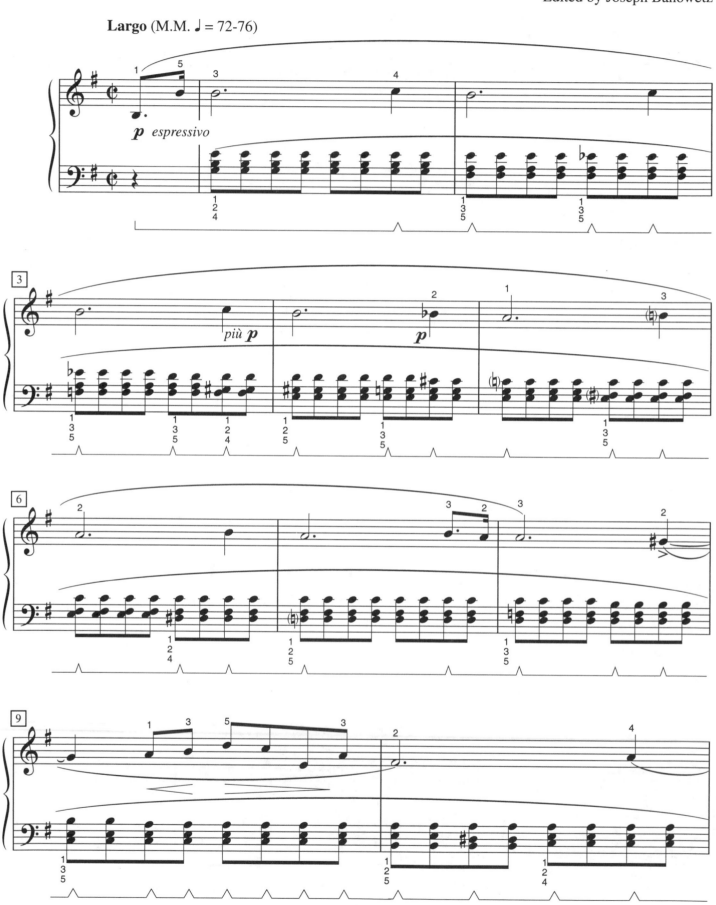

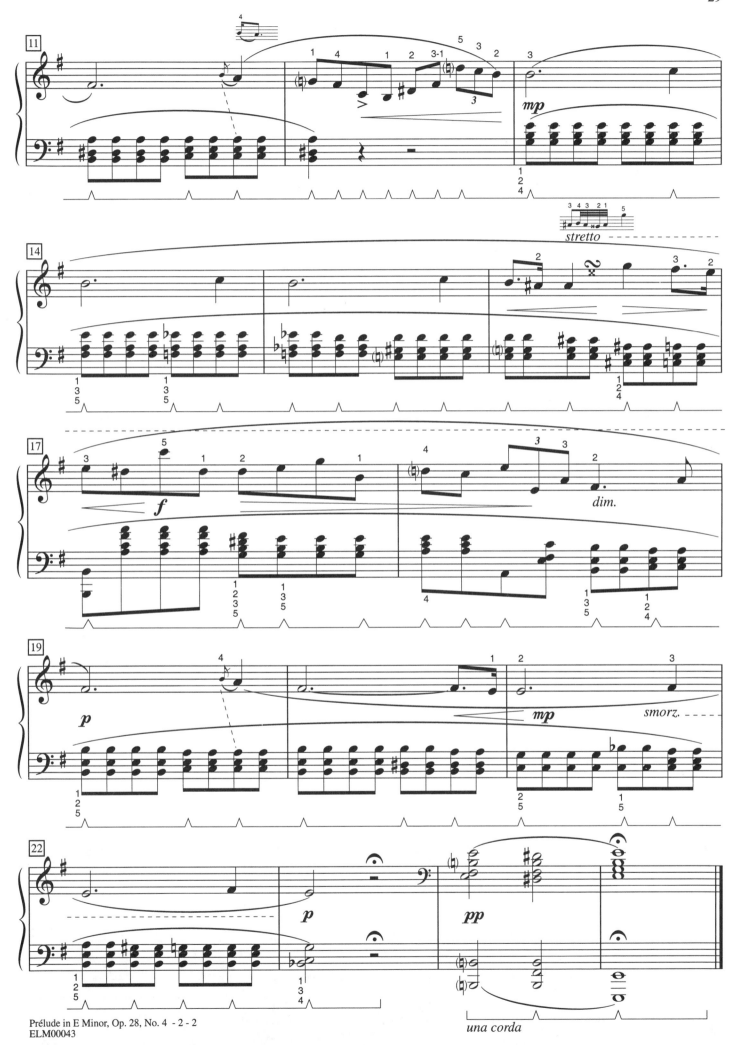

PRÉLUDE IN B MINOR
OP. 28, NO. 6

FRÉDÉRIC CHOPIN
Edited by Joseph Banowetz

PRÉLUDE IN A MAJOR

OP. 28, NO. 7

FRÉDÉRIC CHOPIN
Edited by Joseph Banowetz

Andantino (M.M. ♩ = 88-92)

* Many performers have difficulty in playing this large chord without breaking. (Simply omitting the lower A sharp is not a good solution!)
Rolling the chord slowly is one possible solution. The following facilitation sounds well also, provided care is taken to catch the lower notes
of the chord in a clean pedal change, then hold the pedal while the upper notes of the chord are played.

PRÉLUDE IN C MINOR
OP. 28, NO. 20

FRÉDÉRIC CHOPIN
Edited by Joseph Banowetz

Prélude in C Minor, Op. 28, No. 20 - 1 - 1
ELM00043

WALTZ IN D-FLAT MAJOR
OP. 64, NO. 1

FRÉDÉRIC CHOPIN
Edited by Joseph Banowetz

Molto vivace (M.M. ♩. = 72-80)

*Chopin did not indicate a trill in the original manuscript. (See page 39 for the manuscript facsimile.)

* The F is tied to the last quarter of the first ending.

Waltz in D-Flat Major,
Op. 64, No. 1 - 5 - 2
ELM00043

36

Waltz in D-Flat Major,
Op. 64, No. 1 - 5 - 4
ELM00043

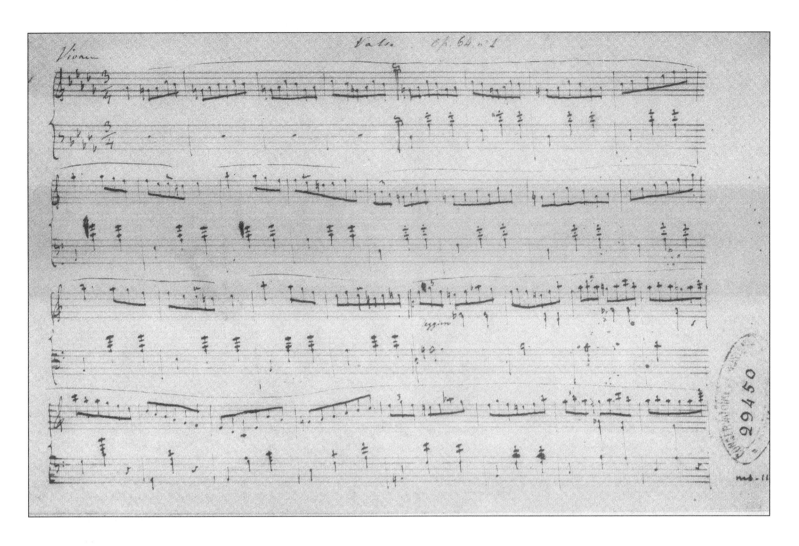

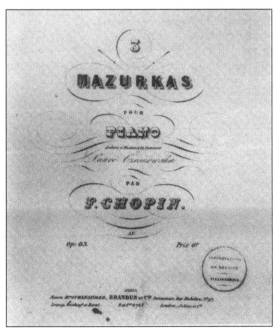

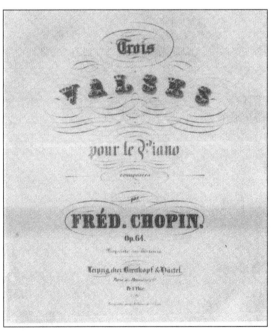

Works completed and published in 1847: original album manuscript of page 1, of the *Waltz in D-flat Major,* No. 1, from the Waltzes, Op. 64, dedicated to Countess Delfina Potocka. Paris, Bibliothéque Nationale since 1946 (formerly in the Bibliothéque du Conservatoire de Musique).

WALTZ IN C-SHARP MINOR
OP. 64, NO. 2

FRÉDÉRIC CHOPIN
Edited by Joseph Banowetz

Tempo giusto (M.M. ♩ = 120-126)

---

* Many of Chopin's small notes (appoggiaturas) should be placed on, not before, the beat. If the performer wishes to do so here, the following realization is possible. In any case, the small notes in this and similar passages should be played lightly and rapidly.

Waltz in C-Sharp Minor
Op. 64, No. 2 - 8 - 4
ELM00043

Waltz in C-Sharp Minor
Op. 64, No. 2 - 8 - 6
ELM00043

Waltz in C-Sharp Minor
Op. 64, No. 2 - 8 - 7
ELM00043

Waltz in C-Sharp Minor
Op. 64, No. 2 - 8 - 8
ELM00043

WALTZ IN B MINOR
OP. 69, NO. 2

FRÉDÉRIC CHOPIN
Edited by Joseph Banowetz

Moderato (M.M. ♩ = 132-138)

Waltz in B Minor,
Op. 69, No. 2 - 4 - 2
ELM00043

50

Waltz in B Minor,
Op. 69, No. 2 - 4 - 4
ELM00043

WALTZ IN A MINOR

OP. POSTH.

FRÉDÉRIC CHOPIN
Edited by Joseph Banowetz

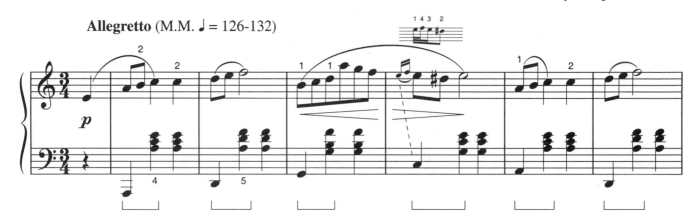

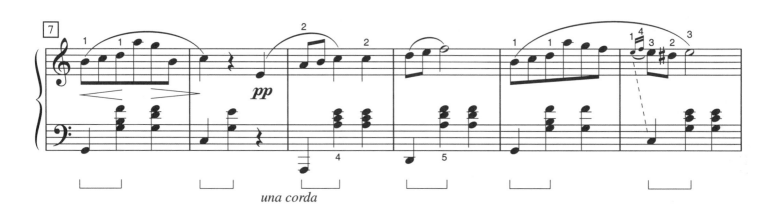

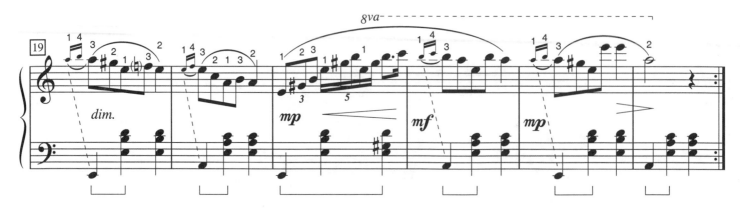

Waltz in A Minor, Op. Posth. - 2 - 1
ELM00043

VALSE MÉLANCOLIQUE IN F-SHARP MINOR

KK ANH. IA/7

FRÉDÉRIC CHOPIN
Edited by Joseph Banowetz

* Although groups of small notes in Chopin's music are often played on the beat, doing so in this case would create an ugly clash of harmonies.

Valse Mélancolique in F-Sharp Minor,
KK ANH. IA/7 - 5 - 2
ELM00043

56

Valse Mélancolique in F-Sharp Minor,
KK ANH. IA/7 - 5 - 4
ELM00043

58

Valse Mélancolique in F-Sharp Minor,
KK ANH. IA/7 - 5 - 5
ELM00043

Frédéric Chopin, bust, left profile. Pencil drawing by E. Radziwill, 1829, in the Antonin album, page 32. Warsaw, Chopin Society Museum.

Frédéric Chopin. Portrait in oils by A. Scheffer. Musée du Château de Versailles.

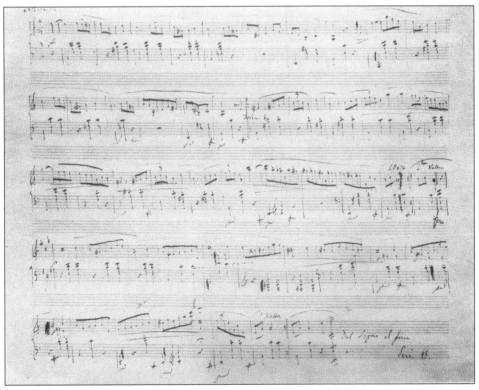

Original manuscript of the *Mazurka in A Minor,* Op. 67, No. 4 (WN59), Paris 1846 or 1848 (the date written in Chopin's handwriting is unclear). Vienna, Gesellschaft der Musikfreunde (donated by J. Brahms).

Frédéric Chopin. Photograph by L. A. Bisson, Paris, 1849. Reproduced from a plate made from the original photograph before World War II. The original was lost with the State Art collection in Warsaw after 1939. Warsaw, Chopin Society Photographic Library.